DARIEN

WOLVES OF THE RISING SUN #6

KENZIE COX

Published by Bayou Moon Press, LLC, 2015.

This is a work of fiction. Similarities to real people, places, or events are entirely coincidental.

Darien: WOLVES OF THE RISING SUN #6
First edition.

Copyright © 2015 Kenzie Cox.
Written by Kenzie Cox.

Join the Packs of the Mating Season

The mating moon is rising…

Wherever that silver light touches, lone male werewolves are seized by the urge to find their mates. Join these six packs of growly alpha males (with six-packs!) as they seek out the smart, sassy women who are strong enough to claim them forever.

The "Mating Season" werewolf shifter novellas are brought to you by six authors following the adventures of six different packs. Each novella is the story of a mated pair (or trio!) with their Happily Ever After. Enjoy the run!

Learn more at thematingseason.com

Darien: Wolves of the Rising Sun

His wolf has already chosen…

Darien Davenne is a man of honor. And when he comes across Thea Johnson, the woman recovering from a traumatic kidnapping, he promises to protect her. But who's going to protect her from him when everything in him longs to make her his mate?

Thea Johnson's world has been turned upside down. All she wants is some quiet time in the bayou to recover. Instead, she gets sexy Darien Davenne, a wolf in gentlemen's clothing. But he might not be the only threat. With more than just her heart on the line, she'll need to find a way to survive if she wants her happily-ever-after.

Sign up for Kenzie's newsletter here at www.kenziecox.com. Do you prefer text messages? Sign up for text alerts! Just text SHIFTERSROCK to 24587 to register.

CHAPTER 1
DARIEN

Sweat soaked through my T-shirt as I tightened the last bolt on the chopper, but it wasn't the punishing South Louisiana sun that made me heated. It was the long legs of the blond beauty lounging on my front porch, her feet up on the railing and a tall glass of iced tea in her hand. The urge to run one of those ice cubes over her luscious body hit me hard. My gut clenched as I imagined her naked body stretched out beside me on my bed.

Christ, man. Get a fucking grip.

For the past week, Thea had been staying at the resort my brothers and I owned while she recovered from a traumatic kidnapping. Lusting after her while tuning up my motorcycle was beyond the pale. The woman needed a safe place to get her head on straight. Dealing with my bullshit was the last thing she should have to worry about.

If only she weren't so fucking gorgeous.

I turned away from the cabin and focused on my bike. Then I let out a humorless huff of laughter. The only reason I was out in the hot sun was because Thea was sitting on my porch swing, and for whatever reason, I couldn't seem to stay away.

"Want some?" she called.

I twisted and eyed her. She was standing at the bottom of the step, holding out her glass.

My lips twitched into a smile as something close to pleasure tingled in my chest. Just having her there was enough. "Sure."

"Come sit with me in the shade. It's brutal out today." She pulled her freshly dyed blond locks off her neck and craned her head to the side, taking advantage of the mild breeze.

It did nothing to cool me though. The humidity was bordering full-on swamp mode. And watching her... Damn, I needed an ice-cold shower. But I wasn't going to pass on her invitation. Wiping my brow with the rag I kept in my back pocket, I took a seat next to her on the swing, sucked down a third of the contents of her glass, and then held it out to her. "Thanks. I needed that."

She shook her head, waving my hand away. "You keep it. There's more inside."

I smiled lazily, loving that she'd been comfortable enough to make herself at home in my cabin. A week and a half ago, she'd spent three days in a human cage while her captors made plans to sell her to the slave trade. My brother Silas and his mate, Hannah, had rescued her before the bastards could set the rest of their plan in motion. And even though she hadn't been physically harmed, she was still recovering from the mental trauma.

"I was thinking maybe it's time I left you alone," she said, staring out at the tree line to the left. "Hannah's old cabin is available. Now that she and Silas have officially moved in together, she said I could stay there as long as I need to."

"Is that what you want to do?" I asked, feeling a strange ache in my chest.

She shrugged, still not looking at me.

"Thea?"

She finally turned and reluctantly met my gaze, unable to hide the touch of panic swimming in her dark eyes.

"You don't have to go anywhere. Not until you're good and ready, okay?"

"I can't stay forever, Darien," she said, some conviction finding its way into her tone.

"Sure you can. I don't mind." In fact, I was enjoying it entirely too much. The second night Thea had been with us, I'd been returning from a night out with the guys just after one in the morning and found her on Hannah's porch, hyperventilating. She'd said it was just a nightmare and that she was fine. But the smudges under her eyes, her pasty-white skin, and her haunted expression hadn't let me leave her alone.

Instead, I'd invited her to my cabin for a drink. She'd glanced once at the empty cabin she'd been staying in and then quickly agreed. But when we got back to my place, instead of having a drink, she'd curled up on the couch and gone to sleep.

Two hours later, she'd woken up screaming, scaring the shit out of me. And I'd done the only thing I could think of. I sat with her, holding her until she settled down, and then offered her my bed. After a little coaxing, she'd agreed. But when I'd tried to leave to take the couch, she'd asked if I'd hold her until she fell asleep. Not knowing what else to do, I'd laid down and wrapped her in my arms. We'd both fallen asleep quickly, and dammit, it was the best night of sleep I'd ever had.

She'd stayed with me every night since then. Just sleeping. The nightmares hadn't completely disappeared, but they were tapering off. Last night she'd only woken up once instead of the usual two or three times.

"Okay, but I should probably make plans to go back home soon." Thea's voice hitched as if she was having trouble getting the words out.

"You don't have to do anything you don't want to do." Unable to help myself, I brushed my knuckle gently over her soft cheek. "You can stay as long as you want. And if you need anything from your place, Wren can pick it up on his way home from work."

Wren was my youngest brother and a chef up in New Orleans where Thea had an apartment.

"That's too much trouble. I can't—"

I pressed my fingers to her lips and said, "It's not. We're happy to help and we like that you're here."

"*We*?" She raised her eyebrows as her glossy pink lips twitched.

"Yeah. We. Me and Hannah. I don't know about Silas or Wren, but no one cares much about what they think." I winked at her.

"In that case"—she sent me a shy, sweet smile—"I might put together a list."

"Good." I finished off the tea and then stood. "Want a refill?"

She hopped up and grabbed the glass. "I'll take care of it. It's the least I can do."

I shook my head as I watched her disappear into my cabin. She didn't have to do a damn thing. Getting to hold her at night was more than I deserved.

CHAPTER 2

THEA

After days of barely being able to function, I was starting to feel like myself again. Thank the heavens Darien didn't mind my staying, because the thought of going home, back to my lonely apartment in New Orleans, was terrifying. The first few nights I'd been here, I'd woken up drenched in sweat, my heart thundering and my fingers aching from clenching the sheets. Getting a restful night's sleep had been out of the question.

But then Darien Davenne happened. I

didn't know why, but I'd instantly felt comfortable with him. Safe. Cherished even. The way he held me at night, kept me beside him tucked in his arms, all while remaining the perfect gentleman, it was almost unbelievable.

I'd never met anyone like him before. Every other man I'd had a passing interest in had been too busy trying to get in my pants. The faster the better.

Of course, it wasn't like I was dating Darien. And I could hardly be considered the catch of the century. Waking up screaming with tears streaking my face was the opposite of sexy. He was just a compassionate man helping out Hannah's friend.

Not that I knew any men who willingly shared their beds with a woman they weren't sleeping with. He was a mystery. And I really wanted to peel back his layers to uncover what made him tick. I was fascinated. All in. But I'd have to get my shit together first. Being a basket case wasn't on my agenda.

I glanced out the window at the man in question, watched him tinker with his motorcycle again, and smiled to myself. He was something else. Tall; dark hair; expressive, dark eyes; and tribal tattoos covering both of his muscular arms. The man was straight-up gorgeous, with just a slight edge of roughness about him. He had the kind of looks that would be dangerous if all he cared about was himself. Thankfully, that didn't seem to be the case. Not in the slightest.

Pushing the window open, I called, "Want some lunch? I can make some sandwiches."

He glanced up from his motorcycle, momentarily surprised, but then he gave me that lazy smile that produced butterflies in my stomach. "That would be great. Extra cheese, no onions."

"I'm on it." Content, and feeling more domestic than I had since I could remember, I hummed under my breath and got to work.

Ten minutes later, I reemerged onto the front porch, holding a tray with our tea and sandwiches. Just as the door slammed behind me, a second motorcycle, an all-black Harley-Davidson chopper, roared up the drive and came to a stop next to Darien. I bit my lip and took a step back, fully intending to disappear back into the house.

But then the visitor tore his helmet off and I froze, recognizing the tall, gangly man with shaggy, dirty-blond hair.

Chase.

What was he doing here? A tiny ball of pleasure blossomed in my chest. He must've tracked me down, though I had no idea how. Hannah didn't even know he was the one I was "not dating." Chase and I had started a casual relationship six weeks ago. Casual as in we'd never actually been on a date, but we had slept together a handful of times. He must've been worried about me to go through the trouble of—

"Thea?" Chase said, his brow furrowed in confusion. "What are you doing here?"

My bubble of pleasure vanished. He wasn't here for me. Of course he wasn't. Why would he be? The only time he'd ever shown real interest in me was when he thought he had a chance to get me into bed.

"You dyed your hair," he added and gave me a nod of approval. "Hot. I do love a sexy blonde."

"You two know each other?" Darien asked.

I shook my head, not wanting him to catch on that Chase and I had been friends with benefits. Although calling him a friend was a bit of a stretch.

But Chase let out a suggestive laugh and said, "Oh, yeah, we know each other. Don't we, T? We should get together and know each other again real soon, huh?"

I gritted my teeth, suddenly repulsed by his innuendo. A month ago, I'd thought it cute, kind of humorous, but now I hated it. Hated the way he was obviously using me. I hadn't seen or talked to him in over two weeks, and he didn't even seem to have noticed I'd gone MIA.

He should've at least realized that I hadn't shown up for my shifts at the corner coffee shop I worked at and that he frequented almost daily. "Sorry," I said, my tone dismissive. "I think I'm busy."

His cat-that-ate-the-canary grin vanished and he straightened, a flash of irritation flickering through his eyes. "Busy? Since when?"

Heat climbed up my neck and stung my cheeks as embarrassment set in. "Since now."

I chanced a glance at Darien and forced myself not to cringe at the judgment I saw there. He was staring at Chase with one eyebrow arched and his lips pressed into a hard line.

"What?" Chase asked him.

"Maybe I should give you two a minute," Darien said, moving toward me and the house.

Chase shrugged. "Doesn't matter, man. She's just some chick who's spent some time in my bed. There's nothing special here."

Darien stopped in his tracks, his dark eyes searching mine.

Two weeks ago, I'd have been hurt by the disrespectful way Chase was talking about me. But today? I was pissed. "Excuse me," I said to Darien and stepped off the porch, standing face-to-face with Chase. "Some chick? That's pretty rude. Just because I didn't jump at the chance to get sweaty with you after I haven't heard from you in over two weeks doesn't give you license to be an ass. Maybe you should consider treating your lovers with a little more respect if you want to continue to 'know' them."

"Hey!" He threw his hands up. "I told you

that first night I wasn't boyfriend material. There was no obligation to call or check in." He shot a look at Darien over my head. "This is why I don't do girlfriends. Too many rules." He returned his attention to me. "I can't be blamed because you females have a hard time not falling for me."

I stared at him, my mouth hanging open. *You females? No obligation? Too many rules?* What a complete jackass. What the hell had I been thinking? I barely recognized the girl I'd been before the abduction. I'd been too trusting, too optimistic, and not nearly discerning enough. The last thing I wanted to do was waste my time on this asshat. "Don't worry, Chase. I haven't fallen for you. You're off the hook with this one. My only expectation was a little friendship. But I can see that was my mistake.

It's hard to be friends with someone who's a complete pig."

"Pig? Fuck, T. Now who's being rude?" he called. The anger in his sharp tone was unmistakable, but I was already heading for the front door of Darien's house.

As I passed him, I paused. "Sorry about that. I hope I didn't cause any trouble between you and your friend."

Darien's lips curved into an amused smile. "You're fine. I'm sure he'll recover soon enough."

"What the fuck is going on here?" Chase demanded.

I ignored him and slipped into the cabin.

"You fucking my leftovers, Darien?" Chase asked, his tone snide.

It was all I could do to not fly out of the house and slap the crap out of him. God. I'd actually thought he was boyfriend material? What an idiot I'd been.

Darien's reply filtered through the window, but it was so soft I couldn't make out his words.

A pit formed in my stomach. What was Chase saying to him? And what would Darien think about me now? I flopped onto the couch, defeated. Despite my initial pleasure at seeing Chase, he'd actually been the last person I'd wanted to see. The truth was, the only man I wanted to be around was Darien. And now I was just his friend's sloppy seconds.

Frustrated tears burned the backs of my eyes, but I blinked them away. I couldn't control how Darien saw me, only how I saw myself.

And right then, for the first time all week, I felt strong. Like I had the power to reset my storyline, and that was exactly what I intended to do.

I was done being the victim.

CHAPTER 3
DARIEN

"I THINK IT might be best if you go now," I said to Chase, barely refraining from decking the guy.

"But what about the bike? It needs a tune-up. Come on, man, you can't leave me hanging." He gave me his lopsided grin, the one he used to get what he wanted. But his charm wasn't working on me. Not even close.

"Can't right now. I've got something I've got to do. But you can leave it if you want. I can get to it in the next couple of days." Just because he was an ass didn't mean his money wasn't good. And it was a crime to neglect the Harley just because its owner was a douche bag. "You got someone you can call for a ride?"

Chase narrowed his eyes and ignored my question. "Something to do, huh? Wouldn't be that bitch who just walked into your house, would it?"

There wasn't any thought process. No reasoning. No premeditation. Only raw aggression as I let out a growl and slammed my fist against his nose. He went down in a heap, rolling in the dirt as he clutched his face.

"You cocksucker. You broke my fucking nose." His voice was muffled.

"Good." I stepped back, shaking my hand. There was a slight possibility I'd damaged a knuckle or two, but nothing that wouldn't heal by morning.

"Fuck." He sat up, blood seeping into his hands. "What the hell is your problem?"

"You. And if you ever talk about Thea or any other woman like that in my presence again, I'll break your fucking arm, got it?"

He glared at me through watery eyes. "You got a thing for my girl, Davenne?"

"I think you made it perfectly clear she wasn't your girl about five minutes ago. And as for who I might have a thing for, it's none of your goddamned business. Now get the fuck off my property."

He tugged his shirt off and used it to mop up the blood. When he stood, he wobbled on unsteady legs.

Christ. Even if I refused to work on the bike, there was no way he could drive it now. I let out a sigh, pulled out my phone, and touched the Uber app. Thank God. There was a car only a few blocks away. We were far enough from the city there wasn't always a ride available.

"Your ride will meet you out front in two minutes," I said.

"My ride?" His nose had stopped bleeding, but his face was already swelling. He was going to have two nasty black eyes before the night was over.

"I got you an Uber. Leave the bike. I'll get it tuned up and back to you within a few days."

"I want a fucking discount," he snarled, "or Gabe is going to hear about this."

"Tell Gabe whatever you want. I don't care." Gabe was the owner of the bike shop I worked at on and off when they needed an extra hand. It was a good bet that once he heard what had set me off, he'd deck Chase too. One thing Gabe did not stand for was disrespecting women. "Even so, this one is on the house. But once it's done, don't bother to bring it to me again. Find yourself another mechanic."

He let out a huff. "If you think I'd bring you my bike again, you're out of your fucking mind. And if you hadn't fucked up my face, I'd be riding it out of here right now."

I shrugged. "Wouldn't hurt my feelings."

He opened his mouth again, but the sound of a horn cut him off.

"Looks like your ride's here. Better hurry before he leaves your ass." Before he could answer, I stalked back into my cabin, slamming the door behind me.

And ran right into Thea.

She let out a startled oomph and backed up, holding her hands out. "Oh, no. Sorry. I shouldn't have… I mean, I didn't… Crap." Her gaze met mine, and red stained her cheeks. "Busted. I shouldn't have been spying, but after I saw you punch him, I couldn't just ignore it."

I did my best to not laugh. "And yet you didn't come outside to see if he was hurt."

Her eyes widened in surprise. "Why would I do that?"

"Because I assaulted him?" I said, just to see what she would say.

"Ha! He deserved it. The bastard. I'd have punched him myself if I had the balls."

There was no holding back the laughter that time. It burst from the back of my throat as I imagined her taking him down. And what a beautiful sight it would've been too. Seeing her knock him on his ass after he'd insulted her would've been the icing on the cake. "Next time, huh?"

She cracked a smile for the first time since Chase had shown up. A real one that reached her eyes. It was glorious, full of life. After her weeklong struggle with sleepless nights and her subdued mood, I wanted to make her smile like that all the time.

"Is he coming back?" she asked, some of the joy dimming from her gaze.

"What? No. He's gone."

"But his motorcycle is here. It's fine. I just want to know when so I can make sure and stay out of his way."

I shook my head. "No. He isn't welcome back. The Davenne brothers do not tolerate that sort of bullshit." Especially not when he was disrespecting someone I cared about. The thought hit me like a sucker punch to the gut.

That I cared about. Not Hannah's friend. Not a friend of the family. *Someone I cared about.*

Oh shit. There was more to what was going on with me than just finding her attractive or wanting to make sure she was okay for Hannah's sake. No, I was in this for me and the way she made me feel about myself.

"Thanks," she said quietly. "I'm not sure what he told you about me, but—"

"Listen, Thea," I said, running my hand down my face. "I really need to get a shower. We can talk about this later if you want." And because I felt like I was going to jump right out of my skin, I hustled through the master bedroom, right into the bathroom, and then just stood there at the sink breathing.

I'd only known her for seven days.

My heart should not be pounding. And I sure as hell shouldn't be imagining what it would be like to bite her. To make her mine in every way possible. My dick hardened as I imagined her under me, clawing at my back while she growled with pleasure, urging me to make her mine.

My wolf rose to the surface, my pupils dilating and my body aching for the shift.

"Not here. Not now," I forced out as I pivoted and jerked the handle on the shower. Ice-cold water rushed out of the showerhead, and without even waiting for it to warm up, I stepped under the freezing stream, welcoming the punishing stab of cold against my skin.

Something had to beat the lust out of me. If

this didn't, nothing would.

The shower did nothing but piss me off. The moment I dried off and pulled on fresh clothes, I caught a whiff of her strawberry soap on my T-shirt. The one she'd washed and folded for me.

Damn. It made me salivate. Long to taste every inch of her creamy skin. To devour her with my mouth and make her mine in every way.

A soft knock sounded at my bedroom door. "Darien?"

The sweet lilt of her voice only made me want her more. I swallowed a growl of frustration. "Yes?"

"Silas is here."

Christ. Just what I needed. "I'll be out in a minute."

"Hurry up. We have business to discuss," my brother called.

"Hold the fuck on," I snapped, stuffing my feet into my boots. Then I took a deep, steadying breath, strode back out into my living room, and did everything in my power to not look at Thea.

CHAPTER 4
THEA

Darien walked into the room, his gaze on his brother Silas. He cast one flickering glance at Silas's mate, Hannah, and gave her a short nod before returning his attention to his brother. "If this is about that ass I decked earlier, save the lecture. He had it coming."

"What?" Hannah asked. "*You* decked someone?"

"The guy I was… ah, sort of dating," I said.

Silas's eyebrows rose in question as he stared at his brother. "What was that about?"

Darien frowned. "He was a dick. That's not what you're here about?"

Silas shook his head. "No. Hannah got a phone call today that Thea needs to know about."

I snapped my attention to Hannah. "Who was it?"

The pretty redhead was chewing on her bottom lip and fidgeting with the hem of her shirt. "Can we sit down first?" Hannah waved a hand toward Darien's black couch.

I took her hand, tugged her over, and sat perched on the edge of the sofa, waiting.

Darien and Silas followed, but neither sat. They stood side by side, giving Hannah their full attention.

She cleared her throat. "It's about Will."

The ball of panic I'd been keeping contained all week suddenly burst, and I felt like I wanted to crawl right out of my skin. He was the "friend" who'd kidnapped me and tried to sell me to the Russians. "What about him?"

She tightened her hand around mine. "I got a call from Bella. She said she saw him poking around your apartment this morning. Said she saw him talk to your neighbor."

Shock stunned me into silence. Bella was a new girl in town whom I'd befriended a few months ago. She lived a block over and was stopping in to take care of my cat.

"I thought that bastard was taken into custody," Darien said, his voice so low and dangerous it sent a chill up my spine.

"Smoke's trying to track down Fischer to find out what the hell happened," Silas said, steel in his tone. Smoke was a member of the pack with legendary hacker skills who also happened to do contract work for the FBI. He was the one who'd been able to track me down last week. Fischer was the federal agent who was investigating the human trafficking ring.

"They let him out," I said, my voice shaking. "There's no other explanation." We already knew there was someone in Fischer's department who was working with the traffickers. Apparently it was someone with higher rank than Fischer.

Silas nodded slowly. "It would appear that way. Smoke will call as soon as he has any information. Until then, Thea, it's probably best if you continue to stay here. No venturing into New Orleans until we know for sure this guy's either locked up or six feet under."

Hannah nodded, her expression fierce, almost feral, as if she were ready to kill him herself. Maybe she was regretting she didn't do it the first time.

Silas moved to stand beside Hannah and dropped his large hand onto her shoulder. Then he ran it up her neck, massaging. "Relax, baby," he whispered. "If the Feds don't do their job, you'll get your chance."

She leaned into him and closed her eyes as she took a deep breath. "Sorry. My wolf sort of took over there for a second."

"I know." Jerking his head up, he locked eyes with Darien. "I'm taking Hannah home now. You cool with keeping Thea close until we know more? Close as in not letting her out of your sight?"

A muscle in Darien's jaw twitched, but he nodded. "It's cool. I already told her she could stay as long as she wanted to."

"Good." Silas nudged Hannah toward the door, but she stopped.

"Wait just a sec." She strode back over to me, put her hands in mine, and said, "He won't get within ten feet of you ever again. Not with us around. I won't allow it."

I gave my friend a small smile and leaned in to hug her. "Thanks. I'm all right, I think. I feel safe here with Darien."

She pulled back, searched my eyes, and nodded once. "You should. He's good people."

Then the pair left, leaving me alone with Darien. He stood near the window, watching them leave. I sat back on the couch, watching him.

He didn't move a muscle, didn't turn, didn't say a word for what seemed like forever. When he finally stepped away, he sat in the chair opposite from me and leaned forward, clasping his hands. "Since it looks like you're going to be here a while, I think maybe we should get a few things out in the open."

I let out a long-suffering sigh, suddenly more irritated than scared. It wasn't lost on me that before this moment, he hadn't met my gaze or spoken to me since I'd tried to explain about Chase. "Listen, if you have a problem with me, just say it. What I did or didn't do with that jackass Chase really isn't anyone's business but mine. And while I'm definitely not heartbroken you kicked his ass, I don't appreciate being judged."

There. I'd said it. Crossing my arms over my chest, I refused to break eye contact. There was no reason for me to be ashamed. Embarrassed I'd thought that jerk was attractive, sure, but not ashamed.

His determined expression morphed to one of confusion. "Judged?"

"Don't think I didn't notice that look you had on your face when you learned Chase and I had been intimate. And then when I tried to explain, you brushed me off as if whatever I had to say was unimportant. Listen, I know now he's an idiot. But I'm sure you've had your fair share of false starts in your time. I think I deserve a break, don't you?"

"Jesus." He hung his head, running his hand over his short hair. "Dammit, Thea," he muttered and then moved from the chair to sit right next to me. Taking my hand gently in his large one, he stared into my eyes, his dark ones full of regret. "I'm sorry. I never meant to make you feel judged. I wasn't judging *you*. I swear. I was judging him. He's a first class bastard."

"Oh," I said, my voice small. "I thought… Well, why wouldn't you let me explain then?"

One side of his mouth quirked up into a self-conscious half-smile. "Would you believe because I didn't want to hear it?"

"Why?"

He chuckled. "Why do you think? The last thing I want to do is hear about your relationship with another man. Especially one like him."

I stared at him openmouthed. "I don't—"

"Think about it, sweetheart. You've been in my bed every night for a week. Do you know what it does to a man to be lying next to a woman he knows he can't have? What it does to a wolf?"

"You…" Oh shit. I'd been turning him on? "You're saying I'm having an effect on you?"

More chuckling. "You could say that. But it's more than that. My wolf wants you. And the longer you're here, the harder it's going to be for me to be around you and not touch you the way a man touches a woman. So that's why I want to lay some ground rules."

His wolf wanted me. Not him. Disappointment rushed through me, crushing the tiny bit of hope that had formed when he'd said he wanted me. And instead of hearing him out, I jumped up and backed toward the bedroom. "There's no need to lay down any rules. I'll sleep on the couch from now on. I didn't mean to be a bother. Let me just get my shower and get ready for bed, then the bedroom is all yours."

"Thea—"

I slammed the door, leaned against it, and promptly fell apart.

CHAPTER 5
DARIEN

"Fuck!" That did not go at all how I'd planned. How could one simple conversation go so wrong? All I'd wanted to say was that if I did anything that made her uncomfortable that she should tell me immediately. Because with sharing a bed and my wolf craving her, things could get out of hand fast.

I moved to the bedroom door, intending to knock, but stopped when I heard the soft sound of her hitched breathing on the other side. Damn. She was crying. I had to fix this.

"Thea," I said, panic taking over now. "What is it? Are you hurt?"

"No."

I replayed the conversation in my mind, wondering where I'd gone wrong. I'd told her we needed ground rules. That she had an effect on me. That my wolf wanted her.

Oh, damn. I was a fucking idiot.

She'd just had a traumatic experience and now I was telling her a shifter wanted her. A surprising pang of loss hit me, leaving me with a hollow feeling of rejection in my gut. Christ. I needed to get a grip. I couldn't blame her. The only experience she had with shifters was when Hannah and Silas had barreled into that warehouse and viciously brought down Will. No matter how grateful she was or how much she loved Hannah, it was a far cry from opening herself up romantically to one of us.

No wonder she didn't want to share my bed anymore.

"I'm sorry. I shouldn't have said anything. But you don't need to cry. Please open the door."

The doorknob rattled, and then she opened it just a crack.

I gently pushed the door open and poked my head in. "Hey. Are you all right?"

She had her back to me as she nodded. "Yes… I just got overwhelmed I think."

I ached to touch her, to comfort her as I'd done the past week, but I held myself back. Pawing at her would likely make everything worse. "I didn't mean to upset you."

"I'm not upset," she said, anger coloring her tone. Then she turned around and narrowed her gaze at me. "I'm mad. Mad at myself for taking advantage. Mad that I ever gave Chase the time of day. Mad that I let myself believe…" She shook her head. "Never mind. I just need to be more realistic with my expectations."

Confusion muddled my brain. What was she talking about? "Believe what?"

"It doesn't matter."

"It does to me." I took a step forward. "Listen, if you're talking about what I said about my wolf wanting you, please don't worry about that. It's under control. You don't have to worry about me wolfing out on you or anything. All I was going to say is that if anything I do makes you uncomfortable in any way to just tell me. When my wolf is involved, I get very protective and a little possessive. It's part of the territory when you date a wolf."

"But we aren't dating," she said sharply.

"I know." I swallowed my regret and stuffed my hands in my pockets so I wouldn't be tempted to touch her again. "But my wolf doesn't know that. Not when you're sharing my bed."

"Well, problem solved then. I won't share your bed anymore." She turned back around and moved toward the bathroom door as if the conversation was over.

I stayed where I was, every muscle in my body aching to stop her. "Thea?"

She paused just before she disappeared into the bathroom. "What?"

"What is it you let yourself believe?"

She turned slowly, her eyes glinting with frustration. But when she finally met my gaze, they softened, and I wondered what she saw there to change her mood so drastically.

Friendship? Concern? Desperation? God, I hoped it wasn't that last one. Though it was true enough. I wanted her so badly I ached with need.

Taking a deep breath, she closed her eyes and said, "Believe that *you* actually wanted me. You, not your wolf. For a minute there, I actually thought there might be something between us, but I obviously misread the signals."

My mouth fell open and I stood there like a moron.

She gave me a sad smile. "I know it's crazy. And you didn't do anything wrong. This is all—"

"The hell I didn't." I strode over to her, wrapped one arm around her waist, and pulled her to me so our lips were only inches apart. "If you think *I* don't want you, I clearly fucked up."

She sucked in a surprised breath and stared at my mouth. "But I thought—"

I covered her mouth with mine, invading hers with an urgency I rarely experienced. Her hands curled into my T-shirt, hanging on while I licked, tasted, and explored until we were both breathless. Then I slowed the kiss and caressed her cheek ever so gently, wanting to burn the memory into my brain.

"You taste like honey," I murmured.

"And you taste like sin." Her lips spread into a slow grin.

My blood rushed straight to my cock and I groaned. "Sweetheart, you have no idea."

"Show me," she said so quietly I almost didn't hear her.

I pulled her closer, reveling in her glorious curves. Goddamn, she felt even better than I'd imagined. "Are you sure?"

"More than sure." She buried her hands in my hair and kissed me with a hunger that made my blood boil.

"Holy Christ," I said when we broke apart.

She smiled up at me, her cheeks flushed. "You're really good at that."

"I'm better at other things." I backed her up toward the bed, running my hands up her bare thighs until I grasped her round ass. "And this? Damn, Thea, I've been dreaming of getting my hands on this all week."

She raised one eyebrow. "All week?"

"Sure. Ever since I woke up spooning you that first morning."

"Oh. Right." She giggled and her flush deepened.

"You knew?"

"Well, I… Yeah. But that's kind of a normal thing for the morning, right? I figured it didn't have that much to do with me, per se."

I shook my head and gripped her ass harder. "To be clear, it isn't an everyday occurrence. Or it didn't used to be, but it is now."

She glanced down as if inspecting my package. "So it might be fair to say you've been a little sexually frustrated since I got here?"

"A little?" I unzipped her dress and pushed it off her shoulders, letting my gaze travel over her curvy flesh. My breath got caught in my throat. "You're so fucking perfect."

Her breasts rose and fell with her light chuckle, and my control shattered. But it had nothing to do with my wolf. The man in me needed her, needed to touch her everywhere, taste her secrets, and make her quiver until she called out my name.

"I don't think I've ever wanted anything more than I want you right now," I said into her ear, undoing the clasp of her bra.

"You have no idea how wonderful it is to hear you say that," she said, tugging my shirt over my head.

It was the God's honest truth. I'd been with women before. But not like this. Not with this ache in my chest and the desire to know every inch of her before I took my fill.

"You're beautiful," she whispered, trailing her fingers over my chest.

A shiver of pure anticipation rocked me, and I clasped my hand over hers. "If you keep touching me like that, I'm not going to be able to control myself."

"So?" Her eyes glinted. "I might like it if you

got a little wild."

My cock ached for her at those words, and I had to stop myself from ripping her panties off. "Christ, Thea. Don't say things like that."

"Why?" She met my eyes and then pushed down her black lace thong and stepped out of it, leaving her completely bare.

"Because of this." I tore my jeans open, and before they even hit the floor, I had her on her back on the bed, her legs wrapped around my waist. "I want to worship you in every way," I said, as I pushed my tip into her hot opening. "But, ahh, yes." I closed my eyes, drowning in her soft folds, straining to not slam into her.

She let out a soft whimper and tightened her legs around me.

"I meant to do this," I said roughly, and bent my head to take one nipple in my mouth.

Her whimper turned into a moan of approval as she arched up, pressing her breast into my hungry mouth.

"And this." I inched my hand between us and found her soft mound, my finger pressing against her clit.

"Darien." My name slipped from her lips in a breathy plea.

"What do you want, Thea?" I asked, my body straining to stay still, to not take what she hadn't yet asked for.

"You. All of you."

"You already have me."

Her eyes flew open, and her nails dug into my back just before she said, "Fuck me, Darien. Now."

A dam burst inside me, a flood of desire and passion, as I once again took her nipple into my mouth, sucking hard as I slammed into her in one long, hard thrust.

She let out a loud gasp, her body tense beneath mine.

I held still, my tongue playing with the hard peak of her nipple while I waited for her body to adjust to my intrusion. "You feel so damned good," I whispered against her breast. "Hot and luscious, and more than a man deserves."

Her body turned pliable beneath mine as she opened wider for me and started to move.

CHAPTER 6
THEA

Everything about Darien turned me on. His hard, muscular body. His dark hair and lustful eyes. The way he kept himself firmly in control when it was obvious he was already halfway over the edge.

I wanted him to get wild, to take me as if I belonged to him, to make me his. Something primal in me rose from the depths of my being, and I knew then I wanted to be his mate. Craved him in my very soul.

The thoughts only fueled my desire as I met

him thrust for thrust, clawing at his shoulders, letting the delicious friction overtake me, loving the way he relentlessly pounded into me over and over again, completely insatiable.

Then I shifted my hips forward and oh, damn. Ecstasy took over. "Yes," I cried, and everything started to tighten. The pressure built deep inside me, the tide of the orgasm already rolling through me. "Right there," I gasped out. "Just like that."

A low growl rumbled from Darien as I felt his muscles bunch beneath my hands. "Come now, Thea. Let go."

His rough voice seemed to break the last of my resistance, and a powerful release exploded through me. I let out a loud gasp and clutched him tighter, holding on as wave after wave of mind-numbing pleasure shattered through me.

Took me to a place I'd never known existed.

"Yes, baby, yes," he whispered into my ear, and while my muscles were still pulsing around him, he thrust once, twice, and then buried himself deep and groaned as he spilled into me.

We lay there for a long time, entangled, Darien still inside me, neither of us willing to let go. But when our breathing returned to normal, Darien said, "That was beautiful."

I let out a small laugh. "Don't men think all orgasms are beautiful?"

"Hell no," he said without any heat. "I'd say rarely in my experience. In most cases I'd go with satisfactory. Some are better than others, and not all are worth even thinking about again. But beautiful?" He lifted his head to meet my gaze. "No, honey. Not like that. What just happened was definitely special."

Emotion rose up and threatened to choke me, leaving me momentarily speechless.

"What about you? How would you describe your past experiences?"

A huff of surprised laughter escaped my lips as I giggled from pure nervousness.

"Come on, Thea. I told you. Your turn." He traced his fingers over my jawline, tenderly tickling my sensitive flesh. "How do I rate?"

"You're kidding, right?" I finally choked out.

He shook his head, the playfulness dimming as something that looked like uncertainty passed through his expression. But it vanished just as quickly.

Was it possible this gorgeous, alpha male wolf who seemed to ooze confidence, was worried I didn't share his assessment of our lovemaking? I cupped his cheek, loving the roughness of his five-o'clock shadow, and smiled up at him. "Do you have a rating scale you'd like me to use? Or should I just show you?"

Those eyes of his darkened instantly with fresh desire. "Forget the fucking scale."

Chuckling, I pushed on his shoulder and rolled us both so I was lying on top of him. "I'd say my previous orgasms have rated from downright nonexistent to completely vanilla to adequate. But with you…" I lowered my head and trailed kisses up his neck, only stopping when I got to his elevated pulse. Then I bit down gently and slowly backed off, letting my teeth lightly scrape his tanned skin. "It's unreal. So perfect I almost feel as if I dreamed it."

I jerked my head up and stared down at

him. "We're not dreaming this, right? I mean, I'm a little sore, and—"

"You're sore?" His hands went to my hips as he started to lift me off him. "Did I hurt you? Jesus, Thea, you should've said something."

"Whoa." I grabbed his hands. "Sore in a good way. The way a girl feels when she knows she's been thoroughly satisfied."

"But—"

"No," I said. "I like it. It makes me feel alive and a little naughty."

"Naughty." His eyes glinted. "Well then. How do you feel about being downright scandalous?"

My nipples instantly hardened. "Only if you do your worst, Mr. Davenne."

His large hands cupped my ass, holding me firmly against his already hardening erection.

"Don't say things you don't mean, Thea. Right now I'm liable to take you up on it."

"Oh, I meant it, Darien. If you can make me come like that again, then I'm pretty much willing to do whatever you can dream up." I sat up and took his hot shaft into my hand, wanting to feel for myself how much he wanted me.

"Christ," he said, his eyes rolling to the back of his head. "You have no idea how good that feels."

I gave him a half smile and guided his hand to my upper thigh, letting his fingers just barely brush against my heat. "Show me."

His entire body trembled with my touch. He stared up at me, his hot eyes raking over my naked flesh. "Gladly."

Then he rose up, wrapped one arm around me, and plunged his fingers into my slick folds as his mouth once again claimed my breast.

The air rushed out of my lungs. Sensation overwhelmed me. All I knew was him, his touch, his hot skin. And he was glorious.

"Ride me, Thea," he ordered.

At his command, I lifted my hips and guided him into me. He was so hard and thick and utterly delicious. I settled on him with a contented sigh, right where I knew I belonged.

"Feel good, baby?" he asked.

"Yes." I let my eyes close as I slowly rocked my hips.

"That's good. Real good." His teeth scraped one of my sensitive nipples, sending a bolt of pleasure straight to my core.

I let out a low moan and ground into him, needing him to fill me up, take me deeper.

"You like that," he said.

It wasn't a question, but I answered anyway as I curled my fist into his hair. "Yes. More."

Cupping my other breast with his hand, he squeezed and bit down harder, the line between pleasure and pain blurring.

My body involuntarily bucked against his and I gasped. "Oh, God. Again, again!"

Darien clamped down on my nipple once more and sucked. Hard.

"Ahh!" He was torturing me in the best possible way. It was my turn. I lifted myself up off his full length, paused for just a moment, and then slammed down, taking all of him.

"Jesus," he said, his voice strained.

I smiled evilly and rose again until he'd slipped almost all the way out, then grabbed him by his base and circled my hips, teasing just his tip.

"Thea." His tone held a warning.

"Hmm?"

"You're driving me out of my mind."

"That was the idea." I leaned down and covered his mouth with my own and once again slammed down onto him.

He groaned into my mouth, his tongue warring with mine as he devoured me, branded me with his hot kisses, his punishing fingers digging into my hips.

He held me so tight all I could do was grind into him. But I was so turned on that when he finally thrust up into me, he hit just the right spot and I exploded. My vision narrowed, turning black at the edges as Darien continued his punishing pace, thrusting up over and over and over again, prolonging my orgasm while he reached for his own.

And by the time he finally thrust one last time and held me tightly to him, groaning with his release, my world had narrowed to just those wild eyes and the wolf buried deep inside him that stared back at me.

CHAPTER 7

DARIEN

I WOKE EARLY, in that space of time right before dawn when you can almost feel the sun trying to come up. Thea was curled beside me, a tiny smile on her serene face as she slept peacefully in the crook of my arm.

We'd fallen asleep in the same position, and there was every indication neither of us had moved. It was the first time all week she hadn't woken us both up with a nightmare.

The place in my chest just above my heart swelled with pride. There was something about our joining that had given her peace. It made me want to gather her closer, to keep her safe by my side forever.

To make her my mate.

I let out a long breath, trying not to let that thought take hold. Sure, being a wolf would give her the ability to defend herself against the likes of Will and the bastards behind the human trafficking. And Christ, I wanted to. Wanted her so badly I ached for her all over again when I'd just had her a few hours before.

Making love to Thea was like no one else. She held nothing back. Gave me all of herself. Completely open and sweet and sensual. She did things to my insides I couldn't explain.

But great sex and turning someone wolf just because it would make them safer wasn't a good enough reason to mate. If and when I chose someone, it was going to be forever. A true partner. Someone who wanted me for me, not my abilities.

And as much as I wanted Thea, both physically and emotionally, it was too soon. Too soon for me to ask her and too soon for her to know what this life meant. We needed time to see where this thing went. I wanted what Silas had. He'd known for years that Hannah was the one for him. And by the time they'd finally gotten past their bullshit and come together, their bond was so tight it was magical.

That's what I wanted. Although waiting six years was taking it too far. Maybe six months, if she didn't run back to New Orleans for good once Will was put away.

As I watched the first rays of sunshine peek through the bedroom window, my phone vibrated on the nightstand. I grabbed it and read the text from Smoke.

I've got a lead. Meet me out front in ten.

I tapped back. *Will do.*

Then I glanced at Thea. She'd buried her head into the pillow, effectively shielding her face from the sun daring to wake her.

I smiled and, unwilling to disturb her sleep, slipped from the bed, grabbed a pile of fresh clothes, and disappeared into the bathroom. When I reappeared ten minutes later, showered and dressed, she hadn't moved an inch.

"See you in a few, sleeping beauty," I said and left the room, quietly closing the door behind me.

I found Smoke and his mate, Scarlett, sitting on the swing at the main office while Silas leaned against the railing, his arms crossed over his chest.

"Where's Thea?" Scarlett asked, redoing a haphazard bun on the top of her head.

"Sleeping." I glanced at the door. "Is there coffee inside?"

Silas shook his head. "Not unless you got here before us and made some."

"Damn."

Scarlett yawned. "That sounds positively divine right now."

"I was up practically all night going through data, trying to trace this bastard. Scarlett helped. But she's not used to all-nighters… At least not the ones that require reading code." Smoke grinned at her.

She rolled her eyes and shook her head. "Men. Is that all you think about?"

"Not all," Smoke said. "But it's usually right there beneath the surface, waiting for any opening."

"Of course it is." Scarlett glanced at me. "If you can point me to the coffeemaker, I'd be glad to get that started. If I don't get some caffeine in these veins, it's going to get ugly."

Smoke nodded gravely.

"Sure." I patted my pocket, realized I'd left my keys back at the cabin, and turned to Silas. "Key?"

He shook his head, looking just as exasperated as Scarlett had moments ago. "It's a fucking combination lock, remember?"

I eyed the door handle, spotted the numbered keypad, and felt like an idiot yet again. How long ago had they changed that? Last year? And I was just now noticing. No wonder

Hannah was always ribbing Wren and me about taking an interest in the business we owned. I had to do better. After the current crisis was over.

"Uh, Silas?" I glanced at the lock. "Do I have a code for this?"

"It's your fucking birthday, man." He shook his head and turned to Smoke. "I told you we couldn't get fancy with the codes."

Smoke was our security guy for the resort. He blinked at me. "Dude."

"I know. I'll think of something better. Just let me get the coffee first."

Five minutes later, the four of us were sitting around the table with steaming cups of liquid energy perking us up when Hannah arrived and silently took her place next to Silas.

Smoke took a sip, then held up an electronic tablet. It was a map of New Orleans, nothing else. "See this?"

We all nodded.

"Nothing, right?"

"Right," we all agreed.

"But look at this." He touched the screen, and a flashing light bobbed in uptown near the bar where Thea had been abducted.

"What is it?" I asked and glanced out the window toward my cabin. It was exactly as I left it. Quiet, no one around, but suddenly it felt wrong to be away from Thea. And though I knew she was perfectly safe, something tingled in the back of my mind that told me to get back to her as soon as possible.

"It's someone working on a proxy server to make sure no one sees where he or she is going online," Smoke said.

"Okay. So?" I asked. "That's not that unusual is it?"

Smoke shook his head. "No, not exactly unusual, but one this convoluted is. It's bouncing to over ten locations. For amateur proxy users, it's one or two. At least the ones in this area. This one is done by a pro. I recognize the signs."

"Fischer?" Silas asked, indicating the FBI agent who was supposedly investigating the trafficking ring.

"That's my guess. Only check this out." He touched another page, bringing up the parish property tax assessor's page. "That house? It's owned by someone named Francine Wills. Son, Wilber Wills." Another page and this time there was a picture of an olive-skinned man in his twenties, clean-cut, muscular, his shirt open as if he were posing for a romance cover. "AKA Will, the man who Fischer let go."

I shot a glance at Silas and Hannah. Both wore angry expressions.

"So it's for sure him?" I asked. Everyone else in the room had been there when they'd saved Thea from that warehouse. I hadn't been involved then.

"Oh, it's him," Hannah said, clear hatred coming through her normally cheerful tone. "I'd know that bastard anywhere."

He'd set her up to be attacked as well. If he came across her path, there was no telling what she'd do to him… if Silas didn't get to him first.

"Okay, so our suspicion is that Fischer is at his house doing something nefarious on the Internet?" I asked.

Smoke nodded. "That's about right. Either

way, we've possibly found Wilber Wills's hangout."

"We're going in half an hour," Silas said. "Hannah will stay here with Thea."

"The hell I will." She stood and glared at her mate. "This is just as much my fight as it is yours."

He held his hand out to her, but she refused to take it.

"No, Silas. That bastard—"

"I'll stay," Scarlett said. "I'll make sure she's okay."

The petite blonde stood up and moved to put her hand on Smoke's shoulder. "You just make sure you stay out of trouble, all right? Because I won't hesitate to break you out of federal prison if they try to put you back there."

His expression softened as he smiled up at

her. "I'm not planning on doing anything to get me busted, but it's good to know you've got my back."

Smoke had spent a little time locked up after he was busted for hacking some years back, but the Feds pulled him out and gave him a job dependent on him staying out of trouble. He still had a year of probation.

"Always," Scarlett said. "Now come outside with me for a minute before you go."

They disappeared out the door while Silas and Hannah continued their mini argument. I slipped past them and headed back to my cabin to fill Thea in on the new plan. I was almost to the cabin when I heard the screaming and my heart got caught in my throat.

Thea was in trouble.

CHAPTER 8

THEA

My teeth rattled as the car bounced over the rough road, jostling me. Sweat poured into my eyes, and my entire body ached from being curled into a fetal position.

I was in hell, stuffed in a trunk with no emergency latch by a man I'd called a friend. Terror clawed at my resolve, shredding me from the inside out.

My only comfort was the small knife I clutched in one fist. It was the one I'd kept in my boot. A girl who lived in New Orleans needed some way to defend herself. The attack had been too quick for me to reach it before I'd been stuffed in the blue Chevy, but now it was going to save me. One way or another, once we stopped and the psycho popped the trunk, it was game over. He was going to get what was coming to him. I refused to be anyone's victim.

My determination slowly morphed into desperation, and my breathing became shallow as nausea made my mouth water. The panic I'd been holding at bay bubbled up, nearly choking me. By the time the car stopped, I was out of my mind, adrenaline coursing through my veins. There was no coherent thought except survival.

Click.

The trunk opened.

At the first sight of moonlight, I jerked up

onto my knees, seeing nothing but a large shadow hovering over me, and I lunged, jamming the knife right between the eyes of my captor. My momentum threw me forward and I toppled over the bumper of the car, right on top of… Hannah?

I stared into the lifeless eyes of my college friend. The one I'd killed.

"Hannah!" I cried, and when she didn't respond, I started to scream.

"Thea!" A sharp voice followed by strong hands gripping my arms startled me out of the nightmare. "Wake up, sweetheart. It's okay. I'm right here. You're safe."

Sitting straight up, I gasped in a breath, nearly choking on my sobs.

"Shh, sweetheart. It's all right. Hannah's fine. She's safe with Silas. It's just a bad dream."

Darien's voice penetrated my awareness as I blinked, letting the familiar room come into focus. The bright morning sun shone through the open window, illuminating the sparsely furnished bedroom.

Besides the queen-sized bed, there was only one small dresser and a hamper in the corner. Darien's bedroom. The place I'd slept for the past week. Where I'd made love to Darien the night before. I hadn't been taken. I was safe. Here in Darien's arms, right where I was supposed to be.

It had been the same nightmare. The same one that had been waking me up all week. Only this was slightly different. In all the others I'd missed my target and had ended up stripped naked and shoved in a human-sized cage with Will taunting me. Why had I dreamed of Hannah? She'd been the one to save me.

"I'm sorry," I said, my voice hoarse.

"You have nothing to be sorry for." He brushed a lock of hair out of my eyes.

I met his dark, concerned eyes and shook my head, anger pushing out my fear. I hated being the weak female. "I've been waking you up all week. You've got to be exhausted." Shaking my head, I sighed. "I should go back to Hannah's cabin. This shouldn't be your problem too."

"It's not a problem," he said softly and tugged me back down so we were lying on the bed.

It was then I noticed he was completely dressed. How long had he been up?

He wrapped his arm around me, holding me close. "This is what friends do."

"Friends?" I pulled away, suddenly pissed. "After what we did last night 'friends' is the word you'd use?"

"God. No. Sorry. That's not what I meant. I mean, we *are* friends. More than friends obviously. I'm not sure what I'd call us, but I think we are at least friends, don't you?"

I stared up at the ceiling, fighting the urge to curl into him, to clutch him as if he belonged to me. Darien had been like my knight in shining armor, the stable force holding me up this past week. Then last night happened. I had no idea what to think about that. Other than it had been the single best night of my life. If he decided to walk away, it was likely I'd never recover.

My heart hardened at the thought, and before I could stop myself, I said, "But how can we be friends? We barely know each other."

He shifted and sat up, his eyes flashing with frustrated anger. "We may not know all the details of each other's lives, but we know each other, Thea. I know that you smell like strawberries, that you barely move while you're sleeping, that you like tea in the morning instead of coffee, and that you'd rather read than watch TV."

I didn't say anything as I lay there, glaring at nothing. My emotions were all over the place and I was still spun up from the unsettling dream. What the hell was I doing?

He let out an exaggerated sigh. "I also know you're ticklish just above your elbow, that you like to take long showers, and that your idea of camping is room service."

His last statement coaxed a surprised

chuckle out of me, and the huge ball of unease in my gut started to crack. I stared up into his dark eyes and smiled. "Okay, so you've been paying attention."

"Damn straight. Now I think you owe me an apology." He said the words with a teasing tone, but I felt an undercurrent there, as if I'd truly hurt him with my words.

I sobered and reached for his hand. "I'm sorry. Really. What I said? It was uncalled for. Of course we're friends. I think…" I looked away, not sure I wanted to voice my next thought.

"Think what?" There was a bit of an edge in his tone this time, and I knew I owed him an explanation.

"My relationship, such as it was, with Chase was categorized as *friends*. Only clearly we never were friends. I don't even think he liked me. And I liked the idea of him more than anything else. So when you said friends, I sort of went right back there. It wasn't fair. You're nothing like him. We are friends. I know that. No matter what else we are or aren't, you've been a very good friend to me. Thank you."

His expression turned gentle and he leaned down, planting a tender kiss on my lips. Despite the fact there was no passion intended, the connection still turned my insides to mush. "You know you're more than that, right?"

I nodded, blinking back the tears threatening to embarrass me.

"All right then. What about you? Have you been paying attention?" There was a teasing challenge in his tone. "I bet you have no idea what I do first thing every morning. Or what I eat for breakfast."

"You're joking right?"

"Hell no. I want to know if you've been watching me." There was a glint of something more in his eyes now.

"Fine," I said, sitting up and pulling the sheet with me to cover my bare body, feeling slightly awkward that he was fully clothed. I took a deep breath and met his gaze. "You're a motorcycle mechanic when the mood suits you. You're one hundred percent devoted to your brothers and Hannah. Every morning you have bacon, toast, scrambled eggs, and two cups of coffee. You don't have an ounce of fat on you, likely due to your wolf side. Lucky SOB. But more than that, I know you're a kind soul, honorable, and possibly the best lover this side of the Atlantic."

I clamped my hand over my mouth, embarrassed that last line had popped out before I could stop it.

He grinned at me like a fool.

"Stop. It's no surprise I enjoyed last night. So did you."

"Very true. And I can't wait to give it another go."

I eyed him slyly. "My schedule appears to be free."

His smile fell and he frowned.

"Uh-oh. What's with that look?" I tried to ignore the nervousness worming its way in. This was not a rejection. It couldn't be. He'd just said he couldn't wait for the next round.

"Smoke has a good lead on Will's location. I'm going with him, Silas, and Hannah to check it out."

I jumped out of bed and started digging through my pile of clothes for something clean to wear. "When?"

"In a few minutes. Hannah's—"

"I'll be out in two." I ran into the bathroom, threw my clothes on, and quickly brushed my teeth. My hair was a nightmare, but instead of brushing it, I quickly tied it into a messy bun as if it was meant to be that way. And when I reemerged, I found Darien and Scarlett in the living room.

"Hey," Scarlett said. "Have you had breakfast? I'm starving."

"No." I glanced at Darien. "I thought we were leaving."

"I am. With Silas. Scarlett is going to stay here with you. That's what I was trying to tell you when you bolted for the bathroom."

Reality crashed around me. Of course they wouldn't take me. I was a human. They were wolves. I was the liability. They were the muscle. The ones with magical healing abilities. "I see."

"It's for your safety," Darien said.

"I know." I waved a hand. "It's fine. I'm sure Scarlett and I will find something to do. It was stupid of me to think I would be going. Especially after everything that's already happened."

"It's not stupid," Scarlett said, eyeing us. "Mates are never comfortable when their chosen one heads into danger. Devon would've never let me go into a situation like this without him, wolf status or not."

We both turned and stared at her. Devon was Smoke's given name, and not long ago,

Scarlett had been the one to turn him. But they'd dated years ago and there was never any question they belonged together.

Finally Darien cleared his throat and said, "Ah, Scarlett, we're not mates."

She smiled. "Not yet." Then she winked and headed toward the kitchen. "I'll get started on breakfast. I'm going to need some comfort food to get through this while Devon is off investigating with you guys."

"Um," I said, heat flushing my cheeks. Then with a nervous laugh, I said, "Well, if we'd mated last night, I guess this wouldn't be an issue."

He stood there perfectly still, his expression unreadable.

After a moment, I waved a hand. "Kidding. Geez, don't freak out."

"Is that what you wanted?"

"I…" How was I supposed to answer that? He was giving nothing away. The question had sounded more curious than anything else, but I could hardly tell him that was exactly what I'd wanted him to do. It was way too soon, wasn't it?

"Thea?" He raised a questioning eyebrow. "If I'd asked you to be my mate last night, what would you have said?"

I frowned. "That's not really a fair question."

"Why not?"

"Because. Last night we were caught up in each other. Great sex, remember? It's not exactly the right time to be making a life-altering decision."

He nodded. "That's what I told myself too."

"Too?" My voice came out in a small squeak.

He took a step closer. "There's this odd thing about wolves. Some of them can sense when a mating is going to happen. It's like a survival instinct, meant to not get between the two."

"Scarlett is one of those wolves?" I asked, glancing at the kitchen door.

Another step. He closed the distance between us, invading my personal space. "I actually have no idea. But she sensed something, and last night, Thea, so did I. I've never had the urge to mate with anyone before. But if you'd asked me to last night, I don't know if I could've denied myself. I want you. My wolf wants you. I told you before my wolf is drawn to you, and now that I've had you, there's no going back."

If Scarlett hadn't been in the other room, I was certain the electricity sparking between us would've combusted.

"Tell me you don't feel it too," Darien said.

I shook my head slowly. "I can't do that."

Triumph lit in his gaze. "You want me."

I wrapped my arms around his waist and gazed up at him. "What gave it away? The way I attacked you last night? Or the fact I only sleep when I'm in your arms?"

"It's more than that. It's this." He touched my chest just over my heart. "We have a connection. And just as soon as I get back here, I'm making you mine."

My heart skipped a beat, and my entire body filled with anticipation. He leaned down, brushing his lips over mine, and just when I wrapped my arms around him, pulling him closer, the front door burst open.

I jumped back, startled.

Darien only glanced over his shoulder and in an irritated tone said, "Great timing."

Silas glanced between us. "Didn't mean to interrupt, but Hannah and Smoke are already in the Jeep waiting."

"You couldn't have given us a couple more minutes?" Darien all but growled as he reached for my hand.

Silas gave him an odd look, then turned and left.

"What was that about?" I asked.

"Don't know, don't care. Now kiss me before someone else interrupts us."

I wrapped my arms around him once more, and when our lips met, I melted into him, feeling completely and utterly like I'd come home.

"I'll be back before you know it," he said when he broke away.

"I'll be waiting." I forced a small smile and waved as he left the cabin.

"Be safe," he ordered.

My smile turned ironic. "You're the one going off to the lion's den. I'll be here baking cookies."

His brow furrowed, and then he laughed. "Now that's something I'd like to see."

I shrugged. "What else is there to do?"

"Save some for me."

The door slammed and I stood there, not sure what to do next.

"You all right?" Scarlett asked from behind me as she leaned against the kitchen doorframe.

"Yeah." I turned to look at her. "I think I just committed to being his mate."

She grinned and then squealed as she ran toward me, catching me in a giant hug. "You're perfect for him."

"Uh, are you sure? So far I'm nothing but trouble."

She snorted. "That may be true, but from where I'm standing, you're brave, gorgeous, generous, and tough as nails. Do you know how hard it is for women to confront their attackers? You were willing to be the first one out the door."

"That bastard deserves to be castrated."

"No doubt. But the point is, you were willing to be the one to do it. You've got balls, girl. And I like that."

An invisible weight lifted off my chest, one I

hadn't even realized was there as I smiled at the woman in front of me. Maybe I wasn't as hopeless as I'd previously thought. "Thanks."

"You're welcome. Now get in here. We have a pile of waffles to plow through."

"Waffles?" My stomach rumbled.

"And bacon. Extra crispy."

"Thank God. I'm starving."

She snickered. "I would be too after a night of sexcapades."

I stopped in my tracks. "What?"

"Please, honey. It's written all over you. Just wait until after you're mated. It's going to blow your mind."

"Even more than it already has?" I asked, as we sat down at the kitchen table.

She stabbed a waffle with her fork. "Girl, you have no idea."

"Well, as if I wasn't anxious enough. Now what am I going to do until they get back?"

She shrugged. "Eat?"

I poured a generous amount of syrup over the steaming waffles and said, "There's not enough food in the world."

CHAPTER 9

DARIEN

The run-down center-hall cottage on Freret Street was deserted. Overgrown vegetation was climbing up the side and taking over half the front porch. One of the floor-to-ceiling windows was boarded up, and the front steps were covered in a layer of pollen. No one had been there in days. Not unless they'd been using the gate and entering through the back.

"Let's check," Smoke said.

"You think they're really in there?" I asked.

"If they are, it's one hell of a cover," Silas

said.

Hannah put her hand on Silas's arm. "I'll check with the neighbors."

"Not alone you won't." Silas nodded to me. "You're with Smoke. We'll be right back."

"Sure." They took off while I pulled out my lockpicks and went to work on the back gate.

"You've got skills," Smoke said when it took me less than twenty seconds to pop the lock.

"Left over from my military days." I opened the wooden gate, peering into the deserted side yard.

"Special Ops?" he asked.

"Yeah. Marine Corps."

"I bet you're glad those days are behind you."

We rounded the house and came to the back porch, finding it vegetation free and a footprint in the dust covering the lowest step leading to the door.

"Bingo." Smoke held up a small electronic device and frowned.

"What?"

"It's a heat detector, designed to tell us if anyone is in there. But it's not picking up anything. It should at least be registering you and me."

"Are they jamming the signal somehow?" I asked.

"It's possible." He glanced back at me. "We're going to have to go in cold. Be ready to shift."

"Always."

He nodded and reached for the handle, then counted to three. We burst into the house, each of us flattening ourselves against the wall.

Nothing.

Dead silence.

Dust everywhere.

I coughed and Smoke glared at me.

"No one's here." I waved a hand in front of my face. "If they were, they'd be here by now."

"That all depends on who they are and why they're holed up." His tone was all business now, and there was a rough edge to him. One that no doubt originated in the run-down neighborhood where he'd grown up. The kind where no one went anywhere without a gun. It wasn't much different than my time in the Middle East. Between the two of us, I was certain if anyone did show, they wouldn't stand a chance.

"True enough." I waved for him to go ahead of me through the house.

He reached for his ankle and pulled out a small handgun. "Just in case."

I nodded and grabbed the one I had tucked at the small of my back. We could shift, tear anyone apart, but if there were guns involved, our best bet was to have a few of our own.

Smoke disappeared into the front of the house while I cleared the bedrooms. Two were completely empty while the third, the master, was strewn with fast-food bags and dirty clothes. The stench of stale grease and mold permeated the air. I grabbed one of the bags and fished out a receipt. It was dated two days ago. Whoever had been staying here hadn't been gone long.

I retreated and found Smoke standing in the middle of a shabby living room, holding a note. "What is it?"

Frowning, he shook his head. "I'm not sure. It's just a bunch of numbers. But it was left in this." He held up an envelope with the word *Smoke* scrawled across the front. "It was clearly left for me."

"It's a trap," I said and grabbed his arm, yanking him back down the hall from where we came.

Behind us, I heard a small explosion but kept right on going and tossed Smoke out into the backyard on his ass.

I landed beside him, barely noticing the burning in my left calf.

"Holy fuck," he said, patting the arm of his sweatshirt, which had caught fire.

"Jesus," I said, squeezing my eyes shut against the unwanted war memories flashing behind my eyelids.

"That bastard. He knew I'd find that fucking signal."

"Who? Fischer? That other FBI agent? Why would he do this?"

"Because he's a hacker just like me, Darien. We do shit for the thrill. But this is different." He brandished the note still clutched in his hand. "The fucker tried to kill us, and in return for living, this is our prize."

"Is that some sort of hacker code?" I asked, pulling him to his feet.

"Yeah. Sort of. In the community, if a hacker can get past your defenses, they leave an Easter egg or clue in your system. It usually contains both good and bad information.

I snorted. "Clearly the bad was the bomb. And that?" I pointed to the letter. "That's our reward."

"Looks like it. I have no earthly clue what it means though."

"We'll figure it out," I said. "Let's get out of here before something else blows up."

The gate swung open and Silas and Hannah came running through.

"Oh my God," Hannah said, covering her mouth as she inspected Smoke's arm.

"I'm fine, Hannah. Be good as new by morning."

"And you?" Silas said, eyeing me. "You look like you lost your best friend."

I shook my head. "Only brothers."

His brow furrowed and then relaxed as he seemed to understand. "The Corps."

"Yeah. Let's just get out of here."

Hannah fussed over Smoke's injuries, frustrated he wouldn't let her at least dress the wound. "You don't have to keep suffering, you know. I can make it feel better."

"It's fine, Hannah," he snapped. "But if you can decipher this, it would help immensely."

She glanced at the note and frowned. "I have no idea what that means."

"Neither do we," I said. "Maybe it's time to google."

Silas plucked the note from Hannah's hand. "No need. It's the satellite coordinates to the resort."

"Why would—Son of a bitch!" I took off running toward the Jeep. "He's going after Thea."

Smoke was hot on my heels, already calling Scarlett. But just as we got to the Jeep, he stopped dead in his tracks. "Who the fuck is this and where's Scarlett?"

We stilled, staring at him.

"If you so much as breathe on either of them, you're a fucking dead man."

The faint sound of laughter filtered through his phone before it went dead.

He cursed and squeezed the phone so tight I was convinced he was going to break it into little pieces.

"What did they say?" Hannah asked, her tone grim.

A storm raged on his face, twisting his expression into one of pure lunacy. "That by the time we get there, Scarlett and Thea will already have been sold into their new lives."

"He's full of shit," Hannah said, already calling someone else.

Silas spoke into his phone. "Tell Jace and the others it's an emergency. To get to the resort ASAP. Scarlett and Thea are in trouble."

Jace Riveaux and his brothers were our cousins. They lived on the edge of the bayou and were a hell of a lot closer to the resort than we were at the moment.

"And Rayna?" Silas said into the phone.

"Tell them dead or alive. Preferably dead."

My lips curled up into what I imagined was a sneer as I envisioned my cousins tearing Will and whoever he was working with into shreds.

"If Scarlett doesn't do it first," Smoke said under his breath, already reaching for the Jeep's driver's side door.

Silas gave him a questioning glance, but when Smoke held his hand out for the key, Silas obliged and climbed into the passenger seat.

"Hold on," Smoke said as he fired the engine to life. "We're about to make record time back to the resort."

I sat and silently urged him on. The sooner we got there, the sooner I could end Wilber Wills and the FBI's Agent Fischer. No one fucked with my woman. No one.

CHAPTER 10

THEA

"I'm in a carb coma," I said to Scarlett, leaning back against the corner of the sofa.

She grinned. "Don't worry. You'll work it off later tonight."

A smile tugged at my lips as I recalled my conversation with Darien. He wanted me. In every way a man… or wolf… could want a woman. The thought made me warm inside. Not only would I get Darien, the kindest man I knew, I was also inheriting a pack. And I would be a shifter. Strong. Magical. And mated.

"You've got to stop smiling like that," Scarlett said, her own smile widening. "Someone might get the impression you actually *like* it here in the woods."

"I do."

"I know, because Darien is here. But there's literally nothing else to do. Or hadn't you noticed?"

I sat up, my tummy bulging uncomfortably. "No. Because it's peaceful. Full of all kinds of beauty. Yesterday do you know what I saw when I woke up?"

She took a sip of her coffee and pursed her lips. "Darien's ass?"

"No." I chuckled. "Though that would've been a welcome sight. I was sitting on the front porch when I noticed a small turtle sunning itself on one of the fallen tree trunks. And then, a half hour later, a doe wandered into the yard. I swear, it put me at ease, as if the animals were sent just to heal me."

She shrugged. "Maybe they were."

"Do you believe in that stuff?" I asked, leaning forward.

She tucked a strand of her long blond hair behind her ear. "Sure. You don't?"

"I didn't used to. But now…" I got up and moved to the window. "I mean, I never used to believe in soul mates either, but that's what Darien is."

"Yeah."

"Did you know with Smoke? Like right away, I mean?"

"Whoa. That's a loaded question. Give me a minute." She pitched forward in the chair, closed her eyes and—

The window in front of me shattered and I swore I felt something hot graze my cheek. A shard of glass, or something worse?

"Get down!" Scarlett yelled as she tackled me. We both flattened on the ground, Scarlett's body covering mine.

The door burst open, and from the corner of my eye, I spotted him.

Will.

Anger consumed all my lingering fear, and I scrambled out from under Scarlett, adrenaline erasing my common sense. "You." I pointed as I moved forward.

"Well, isn't this a surprise," Will said, a twisted smile on his face. "Looks like we get two for the price of one."

"Fischer?" Scarlett said from behind me,

disbelief coloring her tone.

I glanced to the right and spotted a second man coming through the door. One I didn't recognize. Had she just said Fischer? Wasn't that the FBI agent? Why was he with Will?

"Fuck. Scarlett, what are you doing here?" the second man asked.

"Protecting Thea." Her fists clenched and her entire body started to vibrate. An electric current of light crackled over her skin. "I can't believe this. Did you kill Bax?"

"God no. Please don't shift. Let me explain," Fischer pleaded.

But it was too late. Her bones were already snapping and contorting. A second later, the large blond wolf was on all fours, her clothes torn and discarded on the floor beneath her.

He held his hands out as if to hold her off.

She growled and stalked forward, her hackles raised.

"That's fun," Will said, eyeing me. "But we have other matters to attend to."

"What do you want from me?" I asked, my tone full of steel.

"So brave." He chuckled. "Wish you'd shown some of that gumption last time. It would've been a lot more entertaining."

The dream I'd been having all week flashed in my mind and my hand twitched, missing the small knife still strapped inside my boot. I cast a quick sideways glance and spotted my black combat boots discarded at the end of the couch.

Will followed by gaze and frowned. "You got someone else hiding in here?"

"Why would I tell you anything?" Better for him to think there was another potential threat than to realize I might have a weapon stashed.

Scarlett let out another growl and lunged at Fischer, who sidestepped her and reached for his handgun.

"No!" I cried out and leaped, crashing into his shoulder, making both of us go down in a heap.

Scarlett was on him in a flash, her large jaws clasped over his wrist, and he screamed, the gun clattering to the hardwood floor.

I scrambled to my knees and threw myself over Fischer's body, grappling for the weapon. My fingers closed around the cold metal, but then Will was there and a swift kick sent a sharp bolt of pain through my wrist and the gun clattering across the floor.

Fischer screamed, and more snarls came from Scarlett.

I stared up into the cold, calculating eyes of my abductor. "You think you can get out of this, Thea? Think again, sweetheart."

The endearment on his lips made my stomach roll. It was what Darien had taken to calling me, and hearing it come from this slimeball sent me into a silent, blind rage.

"It turns out our associate had special plans for you. So letting you go on with your pathetic life here with the wolves is out of the question."

"What associate?" I asked, just to keep him busy.

A grunt came from behind us, followed by a crash and a yelp from Scarlett. I wanted to turn and see what was happening, but I couldn't. Not with a gun pointed at me.

"The one who places the girls. Turns out he has a thing for big breasts and wide hips." He wrinkled his nose. "Though I don't know why anyone would choose a plain thing like you. Maybe he needs a broodmare."

"Broodmare?" The outrage in my tone shocked even me. Here he was pointing a gun at me, talking about turning me over to a human trafficker kingpin, and the term *broodmare* was what set me off the most.

"I tried to offer him your neighbor, Bella, but he's already, ah, formed a relationship with your picture."

My heart got caught in my throat. "Bella?"

"Now she's a saucy one, isn't she? Too bad he didn't have any interest."

"Where is she?" I demanded.

He chuckled. "Now why would I tell you that?"

"Because if you don't, I'm going to make

you suffer in ways even you haven't thought of."

He let out a loud laugh. "I very much doubt that, but we can compare notes later when we get to my new warehouse. It has all kinds of interesting contraptions that should excite you."

Bile rose up from the back of my throat, and I once again caught sight of my black boots. They were within reaching distance now, but I needed a distraction. He wasn't just going to let me put them on. Or would he? He'd said his boss wanted me. That meant alive, I assumed.

"Sounds like a real party," I said dryly and reached for the boots.

A bullet whizzed past me and lodged into the wall. I froze, my eyes wide as I stared up at him. "What was that for?"

"Do not move." He stalked forward, the gun trained on me. "I don't know what you're up to, but whatever it is, game's over." He reached into his pocket and produced white plastic zip ties. "Now be a good girl and don't make me hurt you... too much."

Be a good girl. It's what he'd said to me last time, just before he shoved me in a human cage for three days. My back straightened, Scarlett's growls and the commotion behind us faded away, and all I knew were the sinister eyes of my aggressor. This was the moment that would decide my fate.

I was done being a victim.

The words I'd told myself over and over in my dream all week were right there, screaming back at me. What had Hannah told me? She'd escaped being abducted the same night Will had taken me because she'd been willing to die rather than be stuffed in that car. My resolve solidified, and as Will reached for me, I tackled him.

"You bitch," he snarled, clearly taken totally off guard as he reached for my already throbbing wrist.

I clawed at his eyes, making him scream and roll away from me. Deep satisfaction fueled my determination. He'd expected me to be a *good girl*. To do as he said. I was done with that.

"You're going to pay for that." Will rolled and rose up on his knees, the gun now pointed at my head. But I already had my hand in my nearby boot, my fingers curling around the ivory-hilted knife.

"You're going to kill me? What about your

boss?" I asked. "Looks like he must've really wanted me if you went to so much trouble."

"A couple of holes in strategic spots won't faze him." He pointed the gun down and aimed at my knee.

A cold sweat broke out on the back of my neck and my head swam, making me dizzy. A knee injury would be agony, but if I survived, I'd get over it. It was better than being sold to some sick fuck in Russia.

"You don't have the nerve," I said, taunting him.

His eyes narrowed as he focused on my knee, his expression dark with unbridled fury. "No one talks to me like that." He spit the words out, his saliva splattering all over me.

I recoiled, taking the moment to grip my knife tighter. Then I said, "I do," and lunged, aiming for his right eye.

The gun fired, followed by screaming as my knife connected with my intended target. My world morphed into slow motion, and I felt as if I were detached, a bystander, watching myself attack another human.

I was on top of Will, my hand still clutching the knife as he flailed beneath me. I held on, unwilling to let go, unwilling to let him get the upper hand. I didn't even know where I'd stabbed him. All I knew was blood streamed down his face while he writhed in pain.

Then suddenly he bucked, and I found myself flat on my back, the bloody knife still clutched in my fist.

"You bitch," he ground out as he hovered over me, one hand covering his bloody eye.

I narrowed mine. "Looks like you're going

to need an eye patch, Captain Jack."

"Better than a body bag," he said and reached for me with both hands.

Another shot fired, and Will's body arched backward slightly just before he fell forward on top of me, his lifeless eyes staring back at me.

"Are you all right?" Fischer, the gunman, tossed his weapon and pulled the body off me with one hand, all the while watching Scarlett, who was still in wolf form as she hovered over me, her teeth bared.

"I don't know," I said, shaking. "What's going on? I thought you were working with him."

Fischer backed up toward the door. "I was undercover." His gaze flickered back to Scarlett. "This was a setup to bring the trafficking ring down. Once Will abducted you, we were going to find out who his contact is and take the whole thing down. Scarlett wasn't supposed to be here."

"You were going to use me as bait?" I asked, my head throbbing, pain radiating from practically everywhere in my body.

"It was the only way," he said. "I'm sorry."

Scarlett tilted her head to the side, appearing to contemplate something, and then shifted. She stood there, stark-naked, glaring at the FBI agent. "That's against all kinds of policies."

He grimaced. "I was deep undercover. The rules don't apply."

She shook her head. "You've been in this from the start. Always right on the edge of trouble, and when it looks like things won't go your way, suddenly you're the good guy. Why should I believe anything you say? At this point, I'm willing to bet you're the one who killed Bax."

Bax was her mate before he was killed, before Smoke had come back into her life.

He frowned. "I know none of it makes sense. But it will. Soon, I promise."

"I don't think so. I'm done trusting you." She took a step forward, her body shimmering as if she were going to shift again.

Shaking his head, he took another step back and produced another gun, pointing it right at her. "You don't have a choice. I don't want to shoot you, but I will if I have to."

The anger drained from Scarlett's face, replaced by disappointment. "You know, Fischer, up until now I really thought maybe I was wrong. That maybe there was some explanation for what you're up to. But I can't see it. My gut says you're guilty. And one way or another, we're going to bring you down."

The sound of cars skidding to a stop outside commanded everyone's attention. Fischer cursed, then grabbed the handle of the back door. He took one last look at Scarlett. "I guess we'll both have to wait to see how that plays out."

Then he bolted, just as the Riveaux brothers burst through the door, one of them already shifting.

Scarlett pointed to the back door. "One's dead. The other went that way."

None of them said anything as they bolted out the door, but as they did, I heard the faint rumble of the car engine that haunted my dreams. The blue Chevy.

CHAPTER 11
DARIEN

SMOKE SKIDDED TO a stop in front of my cabin, beside a red truck I recognized as belonging to my cousin Aiden. Next to that was a black sedan with Tennessee plates.

My heart hammered in my throat as I crossed the threshold and scented the copper tang of blood. "Thea!"

"She's in the bedroom cleaning up," Scarlett said from the table. She sat with a dark-haired beauty who was dressed in jeans and a white tank top. An FBI badge was lying on the table.

I turned on my heel and strode into my room, instantly spotting Thea by the window as she pulled my T-shirt over her freshly scrubbed body. Without saying a word, I swept her up in my arms and held her tight.

"Hey," she said softly into my shoulder, clutching me with everything she had.

"You're safe," I said, more to reassure myself than anything else.

She let out a sad huff of laughter. "For now."

Pulling back, I stared down at her dark eyes. "What does that mean?"

"Just that Will is gone. Dead. Fischer killed him. But it appears I'm on the radar of whoever he worked for, and that's why he came back for me."

Deep satisfaction rushed through me at her

words. Wilber Wills was dead. He'd never again lay a hand on my woman. "Fischer was here?"

She nodded. "I think maybe we better let Bella explain."

"Bella? Your neighbor?" Confusion took over. "What does she have to do with anything?"

"Will said he tried to get his boss interested in her, so as soon as the commotion ended, I called to make sure she was okay. She was fine, and the next thing I knew, she was knocking on the door, brandishing her badge. Turns out she's been investigating Fischer and the trafficking ring and had been tracking him. She was only a mile away. She had no idea about my abduction, though. No one at the FBI does, according to her. She'd taken my story about being away to visit family at face value. There was no reason not to since we were in contact about my cat."

"Jesus," I said, running a hand through my hair.

"You can say that again." She pulled back and took a long look at me. "You look like you've been in a war zone."

I glanced down at the burn marks on my clothes. "They planted a bomb in the house."

"Holy shit." Her eyes went wide as she started inspecting me everywhere.

"I'm fine. We're all fine. It was spotted in time before anyone got a foot blown off."

"That son of a bitch." Her outrage was almost comical in the face of what she'd just gone through. "Good thing he's already dead, or I'd stab him again."

It was my turn to jerk back in surprise.

"You stabbed him?"

"Yeah." Her lips curled into a brief self-satisfied smile. Then it vanished. "It was horrifying, and I never want to do that again."

"With any luck, you won't have to." I grabbed her hand. "Let's go meet with Ms. FBI Agent."

Bella stood and held her hand out to me when we joined her, Scarlett, and Smoke at the table. "Hello," she said with a kind smile. "I understand you're Thea's significant other."

"Mate, actually." I winked at Thea, pleased when she blushed.

"Oh, I didn't realize… Uh, Thea, you're already a wolf then?"

"No. Not yet. But I will be." The flush on her cheeks brightened.

"I see." Bella held out a card to Darien. "I

suppose you have a lot of questions, but I doubt I can answer them. From speaking with Smoke here, it seems we're all in the dark about Fischer's activities. It's my hope that if we work together, we can start putting the pieces of the puzzle in place."

I glanced at Scarlett and Smoke, who both nodded. It was good enough for me. If my pack trusted them, that was all I needed. "I'll help in any way I can."

"I appreciate it." She turned her attention to Thea. "You have no idea how relieved I am that you're safe. Can we chat later? I'm sure you have some decompressing to do."

"Of course." Thea smiled at her friend. "Tomorrow? Lunch?"

"Perfect." She held her hand out to Smoke. "I'm glad we got to connect. Please do give me a call when you're done running your background checks on me."

Smoke chuckled. "It's routine for a hacker. We don't trust anyone. Especially anyone who carries a badge. Don't take it personally."

"I won't," she said, then grinned. "I'd be insulted if you didn't."

Smoke laughed. "I like the direct approach. I'm sure we'll get along just fine. But out of curiosity, what's the worst thing you think I'll find?"

Her smile vanished and her eyes hardened. "Unfortunately, there's a lot to pick from. It depends on what shocks you most. For most people it's probably what you'll find in my sealed records. Homicide charges, age sixteen."

Everyone stared at her in silence.

She grabbed her FBI badge and said, "Call

me when you're ready to talk."

We all watched her as she strode to the door. And just before she opened it, Wren, Darien's other brother, came barreling through. He stopped short and jerked back in surprise, a pleased smile claiming his lips. "Bella. What are you doing here?"

She stared up at him and blinked. "Wren?"

He laughed a little awkwardly and then glanced around the room, spotting us all staring at them in curiosity. "Uh, I take it you aren't here to see me."

She shook her head. "No. I wish I was." She cast us a quick glance over her shoulder. "I'm sure they'll fill you in. I have some paperwork to do. I'll… uh, talk to you later." And then she took off, hurrying out of the house.

Wren frowned as he watched her. Then he

turned to Thea. "Is there something I don't know about your friend?"

"Yeah. She's an FBI agent. Working the trafficking case," Thea said. "And you know her how?"

A shadow fell over his face, and then after a moment, he said, "I met her a few weeks ago at the restaurant. We… Well, we spent a little time together."

"You mean you had sex," Smoke said.

A flush stained Wren's cheeks, but he clamped his mouth shut, not acknowledging the statement. "Someone want to tell me what's going on here?"

"Sure," Scarlett said, chuckling. "Have a seat. We'll fill in all the gory details. Then it's your turn."

He shook his head. "You're not funny."

"Yes I am." She winked at him but then dropped it. "The long and short of it is Will and Fischer came here to kidnap Thea. There was a struggle. I nearly ripped Fischer's hand off. Thea stabbed Will in the eye. Then Fischer shot and killed Will right before he took off into the woods. The Riveauxs, along with Hannah and Silas, are out there now, searching for any other players, but we're pretty certain Fischer had a car stashed back there and is long gone. Bella is an FBI agent Smoke is going to run a background check on, and if she's clean, we're going to share information and track down Fischer once and for all."

He sat back in the chair. Then he looked at Thea. "You stabbed Will in the eye?"

"Damn straight she did," Scarlett answered for her. "She's fierce. A worthy packmate."

"Mate?"

"Yeah, mine,' I said. "Now everyone get out. Thea and I need some time."

Smoke and Scarlett shared a knowing look, then rose and headed for the door. Scarlett glanced back at Wren. "You coming?"

He shifted his gaze from me to Thea and then back again. "Yeah. I guess so." Then on his way out, he muttered to himself, "Looks like I'm the last man standing."

CHAPTER 12

THEA

"What does that mean?" I asked Darien as he shuffled me toward the bedroom. "Last man standing?"

He laughed. "He's the only one who hasn't claimed a mate."

"Neither have you," I said, smiling.

"I'm about to." He ran his hands under the T-shirt I was wearing, cupping my breasts. "Damn, no bra. That should be illegal. Do you know what that does to a guy?"

"No. But I think I'm about to find out."

"Yes. Yes, you are." He pulled the T-shirt over my head and then ran his hands down my sides and slipped them into the leggings I wore, pulling them down in one swift movement.

"You're in a hurry," I said, my body instantly responding to his touch.

He pulled his shirt off and then tugged me to him. "Do you have any idea what it's like to sit in a car, unable to do anything, knowing you were being targeted by that monster and knowing that if only I'd claimed you last night, your chances of survival would've been a thousand times better?"

"I did all right," I said, unbuttoning his jeans.

"You did more than all right. You were fucking amazing. A true warrior. So brave. And strong. And mine." He stepped out of his jeans and walked me backward until my legs hit the edge of the bed.

I placed my hand on his chest, stopping him momentarily. "Just one thing before we finish this."

"What's that?" he asked, staring into my determined eyes.

"Tell me you're doing this because you want me as your mate. Your life partner and not just because it will turn me wolf. That you aren't doing this because you're scared something will happen to me."

He blinked. Then his expression turned serious. "Thea, I wouldn't be asking you to be my mate if I didn't need you, crave you, deep down right here." He pressed his hand over his heart. "I'm not mating with you to turn you wolf. Though I admit, that part does have its advantages. You've already shown you're a warrior. You don't need me to bite you for that to be true. I'm mating with you because I have to. Because we're meant to be, and I feel it deep in my gut. Wolf or no wolf, you're already mine."

Tears of complete joy stung my eyes, and I smiled. "Then take me. I'm ready."

He gently lowered me onto the bed, his large body covering mine. And then as the world faded away around us, he slowly entered me. When my breathing quickened, and my body tightened, and pleasure made me cry out his name, he whispered in my ear, "I love you, mate."

"I love you too," I gasped out, just as his teeth sank into my neck, binding us forever.

Sign up for Kenzie's newsletter at www.kenziecox.com to be notified of new releases. Do you prefer text messages? Sign up for text alerts! Just text SHIFTERSROCK to 24587 to register.

Book List:

<u>Wolves of the Rising Sun</u>

Jace

Aiden

Luc

Craved

Silas

Darien

Wren

Printed in Great Britain
by Amazon